Time in Transit

Time in Transit

poems by

David Sanders

The Literary House Press
of Washington College
Chestertown, Maryland

The Literary House Press
Washington College
Chestertown, Maryland 21620

Some of these poems first appeared, often in different form,
in the following publications: *The New Orleans Review,
Poetry East, Staten Island Review, Mankato Review,
Stand Magazine, PN Review, New Letters,* and *Sparrow.*

ISBN 0-937692-12-3

For my father,
Edward Rembert Sanders, Jr.
and in memory of my mother,
Margaret Collyer Sanders

CONTENTS

Time in Transit

Dream of the Coal Holds

Past the stand of pines
that barely hides a family plot
where all the stones but one
bear the same last date,

and the slat-gapped barn
perched in its defying tilt,
which, year by year,
becomes more unbuilt,

then right at what's left
of a farmhouse (one supposes)
beached like the ribs of a ship
on a reef of wild roses,

a set of railroad tracks emerge
a half-mile down,
weed-strewn and unused.
Followed around

the eastern bend they come
on a building made of brick,
squat and off to one side,
the top even with the track:

a series of chambers, really,
connected by doorless door-
ways, each room with a chute
down which they used to pour

the coal. I stood there once,
my camera in hand,
with the ghosts of my grandfathers
over from England—

coal men, *collyers*
they were called. I did not
see them standing there
till finally I brought

the camera to my eye
and focused the lens
on the repeating frames
and empty holds. Like friends

at a rare reunion
they smiled shyly or scowled
for the fraction of a second
the camera allowed.

And it didn't seem strange—only odd
that I'd carried them that far,
unknowingly—or wrong
to have seen them suddenly there.

The Cello

The even tremor
measured by the bow
has worked into the wood.
It's sleeping now,

at least as far
as you're concerned.
Not for a song, the cello
sold and turned

into a trip abroad:
Europe by Eurorail
through obligatory fields;
your love airmail

to the faithful who
would not go away;
memories of places
you dared not stay

too long in. Always
the fear as sweet
as a permanent address,
the chance to meet

that stark reflection
in a storefront window
some rain-tinselled night
again. And so

the continental cities
weathered your move
through them, strung
like pictures in the Louvre.

And you returned
emptied of a lot
of days and hours and minutes.
Who cares about

the raw silence now
on your short-lived visits,
if it bought you time
and the distance that elicits?

Dinner Music

I wanted some music for them, the two
who sit over wine and close
the restaurant
with me. Neither knows
the waiters' impatience as I do

sitting at the bar with my bottle of beer
since they can't see beyond
their table's clearing
in a forest of chairs upon
the other tables. I watched in the mirror

and imagined a tenor saxophone
growling in some lair,
in some apartment,
building as if the player
played for himself and them alone,

and I just happened to happen by,
his keyless solo swelling
and contracting,
their furtive glances filling
the silences in his lullaby.

But there is no music other than
that of fingertips
circling the rim
of a glass. She takes two sips,
and then again the pipes of Pan

start up, as airy and unsteady
as echoes finding their way
back to the source.
I slide off the stool and pay
my tab. The waiters too are ready

to have the evening's concert finish,
to hoof it out of there.
Once outside
amid the traffic air,
we, unmoved, let the panicked ring diminish.

Pianos

I saw them as a child
in the houses of people my parents knew,
each one sulking in a darkened room
beneath arrangements of family portraits.

There I'd lift the lip
that pouted over chipped and yellowed teeth
and slightly press the lowest key
enough so that the bass note hummed through me.

I never heard the hours
of practiced torture or those mornings when
dusting hands stopped to tour again
the foreign shore of a half-remembered strain.

So much that wasn't played,
the silence resonating like the dusk
that ushers out the fall, and yet
the portraits in their frames have multiplied.

Furniture now of friends,
undisturbed and undisturbing, the strings
ease further out of tune against
the padded hammers waiting to be sprung.

Short Wave

Long after the lovers have had
their fill of radio requests
and turned toward simpler, unsad
hearts humming in their nests,

and I myself have nodded off
sometime before my oldies show
ended with "Goodnight, My Love,"
as it did last week and two weeks ago,

you're at home with astral voices—
broadcasts of a different band—
pulling in the global noises
that somehow likewise pull you in.

Leaning forward in your rocker,
to ease the tuning dial,
gently, like a safecracker,
until the tumblers finally fall,

you've tuned in to what you want to hear:
idling cars and satellites,
the whole cacophonous atmosphere
sounding like a summer night's

Babel—tappings, flutters, a shrill
full, makeshift orchestration.
In among the high-pitched trill
you move on to a steady station,

a program in a foreign tongue
bringing the Voice of America and a
serious provincial song
to you (a subtle propaganda

providing a touch of history
like an out-of-town but major paper).
Who else listens to our coded mystery,
the atonal music of at least one sphere?

Some minor god who's more than what he does
but cursed and sickened by what he hears?
For him, silence is a far-off buzz.
For you, the air is dark but clear.

Night Work

Not until
the thunder closed in
did I, already
awake by the storm,
prop myself up
and peer past the sill
in the dark. I saw,
repeatedly then,
the lightning light up
the magnolia
blossoms in bloom
like butlers' gloves
surprised to life,
the neighbors' yard,
my car in the drive,
the walls of my room.
Illumination
came and went
like afterthought
thought better of
and left unsaid,
as quick as that.

The thought I had
was that this thrashing
about with rain
and wind, domestic
as it seemed, was
a kind of maintenance—
a breaking loose

of elements,
balance awry
righted awhile—
though I couldn't say
what kind. It took
no time at all
for the thought to pass,
but it tired me.
Soon after that,
the time began
to widen between
the flash of light
and corresponding
ball of sound.
And when again
I tried to sleep
I could, I found.

Not Then, Not There

Headed downstairs from the office
before I started work this morning,
to double-check that the furnace

had been switched on by the maintenance men,
something struck me as familiar
(exactly where before, and when?)

as I smelled the dust-singed air
of the boiler's heat, on the step.
And I saw, as after a long stare

at the sun, the momentary face
of the somber high school janitor
who looked after me half-days

when I was five and let me sling
into the furnace shovelfuls
of shiny coal glistening

from a mound on the basement floor.
After such remembering,
I stumbled on the bottom stair,

and tried with a squint to shake it off,
as if today, in particular, I believed
neither gravity nor light were strong enough

and this slight past better unretrieved.

Box Kites at Nags Head

Cape Hatteras, early 'sixties

Every year, my brothers built a kite:
wood, paper, glue, and string.
Every year the try at flight
was a nervous, tenuous thing.

Before it finally put out to sea
they tied it to a log.
A bottle note, of sorts, part tree,
part architectural flag.

Dim mirages—freighters—crawled the horizon
and fighter jets would buzz
the waves, in training for some good reason
(those years there seemed there was).

But no deliberate plane or boat
ever concerned the summer craft
of log and kite, kept afloat,
aloft, by what they couldn't lift.

The Gulf

Uncanny
how you plunge through
all those small waves,
which sting your ancient skin
exactly unlike flames,
and time your occasional swim
so as to never tire.

So sure
you are to leave yourself
time to walk the shore,
to find that odd shell,
to dutifully scout the horizon
for some southbound freighter—
barely there, then gone.

Still
the minutes lost on this sand,
alone and apart, my father,
are not enough to cure
what nothing here can,
not even this body of water:
salty and buoyant and pure.

Day Trip

We walk through dreams like this:
accepting, unsurprised, a little
distracted, as if nothing were amiss.

Last spring the river rose
and left its flotsam lodged in trees
like squirrels' nests. Who knows

what forgotten betrayal or regret
it would, if this were dream
and not reality, represent?

Or when the river shoots canoes
downstream, past us,
who, wading out, nearly lose

our footing, what lost passages
might those be? Who knows or wants to?
And what guarded messages

didn't I find in the luna moth,
its celadon wings intact though frayed,
lying on the hard dirt path

back to the cabin? I wanted none.
This is no brilliant, double world
of dream, only the semblance of one.

And if we run into a squall
on our drive back home, let's
let it mean little, or nothing at all.

Mayflies

The way the pond popped you'd have guessed
a light rain had broken out—not fish.
Hatching mayflies hugged the surface, a frail mist
that shook the water alive. Their one wish
(if you could call it that)
was to mate
before they died. It had taken years
to come this far.

Years later
what I remember
is not what was said
that quick weekend, or our cottage bed,
but the whiskered tails
and wings like shattered glass,
and the morning after, with its thousands of small bodies
scattered across the grass.

River Where the Lovers Wait

Bats come here to hunt at dusk,
following the paths of insects that loop
above the water. From the shore,
I toss handfuls of stones in the air,
watching the bats dive then veer
from that wrong, unfamiliar pattern:
they, in their way, know better.

Night Falls

Where the lucent underwater knives
of lights reflected from the bridge
pin back the river's weave
like black bunting, it arrives

at the rim in time to fall
in one long silver sheet
that never stops. The continuity,
the gravity of it all.

The falls at night
is all I want to remember here:
the river's gentle, if endless, explosion
turning the boulders below to a kind of light.

Housekeeping

The living pack us up.
Now that we have gone and died
it's comforting to them
to know that we are tucked inside

a box, an urn, or closet
where memories, like dreams, abound.
They tend to the mess
our dying first has left around.

(Letters dried to mica,
clothes gone further out of style,
souvenirs of us
in storage, kept a little while.)

They allow themselves sadness,
drifting near this windy border.
But grief has raked out its embers,
which cool and die among the order.

Lament

There is a funeral in you,
an open grave filled with the tears
of no tears, a procession
of hours walking behind you.
Consumed and clouded,
you cannot see yourself
trying to dance. The days do nothing
but hold you. Each morning
the tired diggers start again.
The drums of the afternoon
lead you to your night.
You turn away not wanting
to see. You turn away
until you are encircled.
Quiet your heel and mourn.

White Dogwoods

The season of buds broken into bloom
we watch progress is a slow surprise.
And yet we start when, there behind

the other trees complete in their green
experiment, the white dogwoods
seem to be those patches of sky

that break behind a stand of trees
edged up ahead by a field or valley
as one approaches the end of a woods.

And though this may be a blurred reverie,
it's hard to consider them a promise
of more than beauty, a preparation

for the usual greenery. We give way
to our constant waning attention
after the papery ornaments have fallen,

a flurry in the warm breezes,
and we avert our eyes from the trees
now simply green, to the white on the ground.

Here, Now

A group of young punk rockers congregate
on the street this still summer night,
looking restless and somewhat lost,
toying with their locks and ideas of lust;
as if nonchalance were an unstudied move,
they don't approve of me or disapprove,
and not a parent, I likewise am not blessed
with the baggage that comes with the child.

Instead I watch them, knowing how I cursed
the Ohio sky that kept me from the wild,
and how we made it seem like somewhere else
with all that one garage band could call forth,
without imagining it would come to this,
for all that it was and wasn't worth.

The Seabird Diorama:
Natural History at Balboa Park

Captured,
they froze,
suspending
animation—an act
denatured,
which lacked
a proper ending,
not this pose:

the mother
never quite
reaching the beak
of the other,
her chick,
stuck in an infinite
yawn;
and us, looking on.

Picture Window

From the chair in the room
in the house on the hill
she sees the world (*a* world)
in the ripples of hills
where the road slips by
and all is green
until night, which is flecked
with lights from the farms
and, if it's clear,
the red, green, and blue
airport lights on the horizon.
It's this she searches
with her binoculars,
the school bus route,
the ambulance racing
through the hills,
the someone crossing the meadow,
the tractor's progress
in a field above a woods
above the top of a barn
and silo, looking, looking.

But closer still
in her own backyard,
which seeps away to field,
she keeps close track
of the birds that flit
from the trees to the brush
by the spring in the rocks,
which the farmer who lived here

(when this was all farm),
in order to clear the land,
pushed to that low place
he used as a dump.
Birds splash in the water
and cover the mud
with hundreds of barbed-wire tracks.
She doesn't see that,
just the focused mesh
of branches and birds
flattened in magnification:
cardinals, grackles,
red-winged blackbirds.

It's the smaller birds,
the wrens and sparrows,
that fly over the yard
and into the window
as if into nothing.
Then she comes running
often to nothing
when the bird, merely stunned,
had flown away,
but sometimes she finds
in the grass below
a bird lying dead.

For if someone stood
outside in the yard
looking toward the window,
he would see himself
among the trees and grasses,
not the woman or the room.

Gossip

These days the chatter turns to friends
who've quit responding to our letters,
a brave but botched attempt at love,
the neighborhood: bulletins that, for us,
preëmpt the evening news.

And though all the time we chide
ourselves for passing on what we've heard
(prolonging by our whispers rumors,
sad facts not even we should know and yet
make sure all others do),

it seems that this is flesh and muscle
and so makes somewhat tolerable
the bones and joints that prop us up:
cold houses we walk into afternoons,
the bulk mail, the bills.

Amish

I still see him
walking his bicycle
out of time
on the tertiary dirt road

and up ahead,
freed of the daytime cringe
of electric fences, the herd
he worked slowly toward

the barn. Like slack reins
slung with gravity,
one strand phone lines
led them uphill.

This was not his farm.
And in the cut crop field
a combine lay
quiet, its giant yield

having earned its keep.
Other hands had gone to town,
each in the market
for a woman to winter on.

And while I waited idly
in my father's Thunderbird,
down the road the car's
stormy rumble was heard

but ignored. I saw
from the back the cross
of suspenders, and, when he turned,
the naked face,

which signifies a single man.

Dressing the Pheasant

After the knife hit the craw
of the bird gone stiff and cool
with ice and time in transit,
I removed the seeds, still whole,

from below the cocked head
and fingered them like beads,
one prayer a piece, as if grain
picked from the gullet of a bird

were of greater grace than if not,
in a hunter's boot, let's say,
shook out and left to grow,
or before the bird was shot,

if hours had passed and the seeds
had broken down and turned
into the spectrum of feathers
that rose out of its nest of weeds. . .

But when all the seeds that filled
that sack inside the bird—
the rest of the broken string—
slipped out and spilled,

I could not make them more
than they were:
undigested and wet on a paper
bought for the occasion, the chore.

John Porter Produce

This is the shower
that every day settles the dust.
In less than an hour
it's passed; then, a crust
of mud coats everything.

Since now it's raining,
duck inside. And though the rain won't stop,
it turns into a mercurial drop
in a bucket. Near the grapes,
a cat naps.

On the wall, a calendar
noting the days the lunar phases appear
is open to June
of last year.
Not that time stopped then,

or slowed, it's just that it has gone
as quietly as their game of dominoes,
which anyone might lose.
Eggs and fruit are what the days produce.
Each old man knows

the weight and cost of all
the goods by holding them in hand. Still, the one
who's just played his turn
weighs them on the scale
for a stranger who happened in

while the fruit sat ripening.
Step outside—
the rain has quit and the mud has nearly dried.
The sun is out
and the air, unlike before, is not so dirty.

Inside the bag, the fruit
is fresh, almost bitter, and gritty.

David Sanders was born and raised in northeastern Ohio. He received his BFA in Creative Writing from Bowling Green State University and his MFA from the University of Arkansas, where he was the recipient of the Christopher McKean Award for Poetry, the Kenneth Patchen Poetry Award, the Dudley Fitts Translation Award, and a Lily Peter Fellowship. He is the director of the Purdue University Press and teaches poetry at the university.

COLOPHON

This edition of TIME IN TRANSIT designed by William C. Bowie in Minion type is limited to three hundred copies of which twenty-six have been lettered A–Z and signed by the author.

———

The winged gear used here as a dingbat was adapted by Chiquita Babb from a stencil on the face of a German Art Deco travel clock.